Robby Rat and Ricky Rabbit

Om KIDZ
An imprint of Om Books International

Om Kidz | Om Books International

Reprinted in 2023

Corporate & Editorial Office
A-12, Sector 64, Noida 201 301
Uttar Pradesh, India
Phone: +91 120 477 4100
Email: editorial@ombooks.com
Website: www.ombooksinternational.com

Sales Office
107, Ansari Road, Darya Ganj
New Delhi 110 002, India
Phone: +91 11 4000 9000
Email: sales@ombooks.com
Website: www.ombooks.com

ISBN: 978-93-52760-33-6

Printed in India

10 9 8 7 6 5 4 3 2

Robby Rat and Ricky Rabbit

Paste your photograph here

My name is

Robby Rat and **Ricky Rabbit** live in their burrows.

Their burrows are in
a farm under a **rock.**

Every morning, **Robby Rat** and **Ricky Rabbit rush** out to gather food.

Robby Rat gathers **rice.**

Ricky Rabbit gathers carrots.

One night, it **rains** very hard.

Robby Rat's burrow gets destroyed.

He goes **running** to

Ricky Rabbit for help.

However, **Ricky Rabbit** behaves **rudely** and is not **ready** to help **Robby Rat.**

He asks him to
return to the farm.

Robby Rat finds a tree.
It has a **round rubber** tyre
hanging from a **rope.**
Robby Rat reaches it and
rests inside the **ring** of the tyre.

A month goes by. Next month, it **rains** hard again. This time, **Robby Rat** is prepared. He stays safe as his new home is made out of **rubber.**

It **rains** harder than the last month and **Ricky Rabbit's** burrow gets destroyed.

He comes **running** to
Robby Rat for help.

Robby Rat is **reading.**
He sees **Ricky Rabbit**
waiting outside.
He **remembers** what
Ricky Rabbit had done.

Ricky Rabbit is wet and shivering.

His eyes and nose are **red.**

Robby Rat feels sorry for him and lets him in.

Ricky Rabbit wraps himself up in a **rug** and feels warm inside **Robby Rat's** home.

He feels **really** ashamed
of his previous actions.

Ricky Rabbit says
sorry to **Robby Rat.**
They become friends.

They decide to help each other in times of need. For them, it is the **right** thing to do.

Robby Rat and **Ricky Rabbit** start gathering food together. They become **rich** and live happily over the years.

Know your words

Naming words

Robby	rock	ring
Ricky	rubber	room
rat	rope	rug
rabbit		

Describing words

rudely	right	round
red		

Doing words

remembers	reading	rains
reaches	return	rests
running		

Sight words

really	ready

Help Robby Rat reach Ricky Rabbit's burrow.

Join the dots and colour the carrot for Ricky Rabbit.

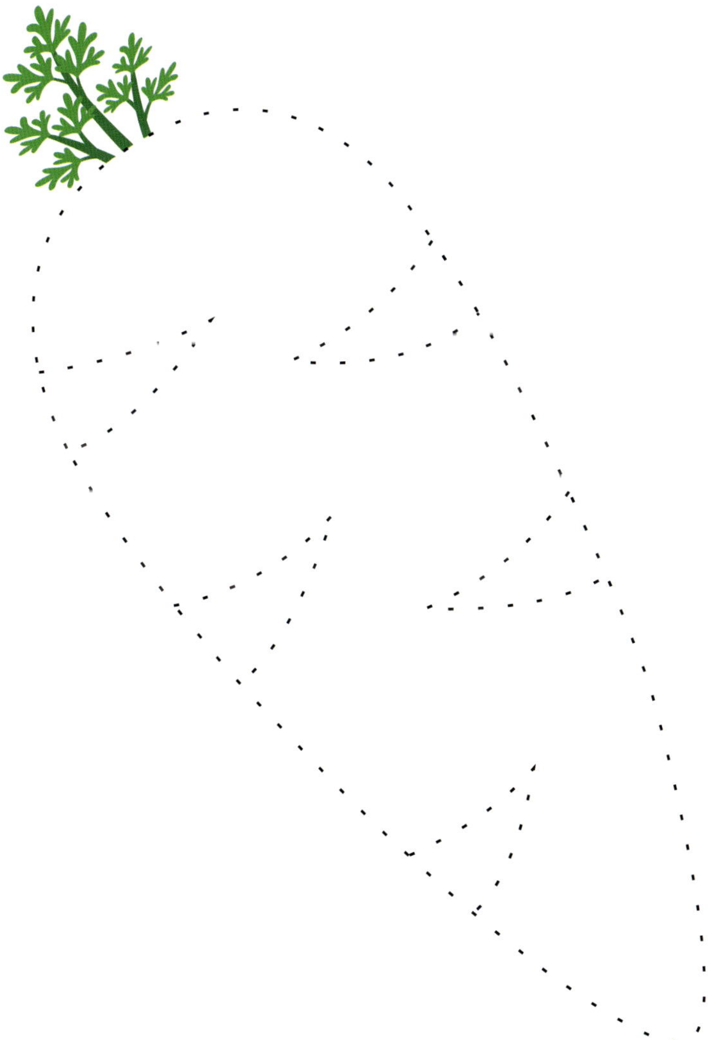

Find the below words in the word search.

I	R	E	S	P	T	K	X
P	N	E	P	Z	T	A	C
W	R	R	A	X	H	J	R
H	U	U	A	L	A	U	I
E	G	V	L	I	L	W	G
C	Q	G	S	E	S	Y	H
V	W	R	U	H	D	E	T
A	R	E	D	Z	Q	E	S

REALLY

RAISES

RULE

RIGHT

RUG

RED